TO RYLAN ROBERT BARNES.
WISHING YOU LOTS OF MONSTROUSLY FUN ADVENTURES!
LOVE, YOUR GREAT-UNCLE. —D.W. L.

FOR MY DAD, AND ALL THE PLAYTIME MEMORIES! —J. C.

Library of Congress Cataloging-in-Publication Data:

LaRochelle, David, author.
Monster & son / by David LaRochelle ; illustrations by Joey Chou.
pages cm
Summary: A monster and his son fill their day with rough and rowdy fun.
ISBN 978-1-4521-2937-2 (alk. paper)
1. Monsters—Juvenile fiction. 2. Fathers and sons—Juvenile fiction.
3. Stories in rhyme. [1. Stories in rhyme. 2. Monsters—Fiction. 3. Fathers and sons—Fiction.]
I. Chou, Joey, illustrator. II. Title. III. Title: Monster and son.

PZ8.3.L327Mo 2016
813.54—dc23

2013046721

Manufactured in China.

Design by Kristine Brogno.
Typeset in Peral and Soto.
The illustrations in this book were rendered digitally.

10 9 8 7 6 5 4 3 2 1

Chronicle Books LLC
680 Second Street, San Francisco, California 94107

Chronicle Books—we see things differently.
Become part of our community at www.chroniclekids.com.

MONSTER & SON

By DAVID LAROCHELLE

ILLUSTRATED By JOEY CHOU

chronicle books · san francisco

You woke me with a monstrous roar,
my brave and fearless son,

and led the way that filled our day
with rough and rowdy fun.

Our game of catch was wild and fast,
our game of tag was too.

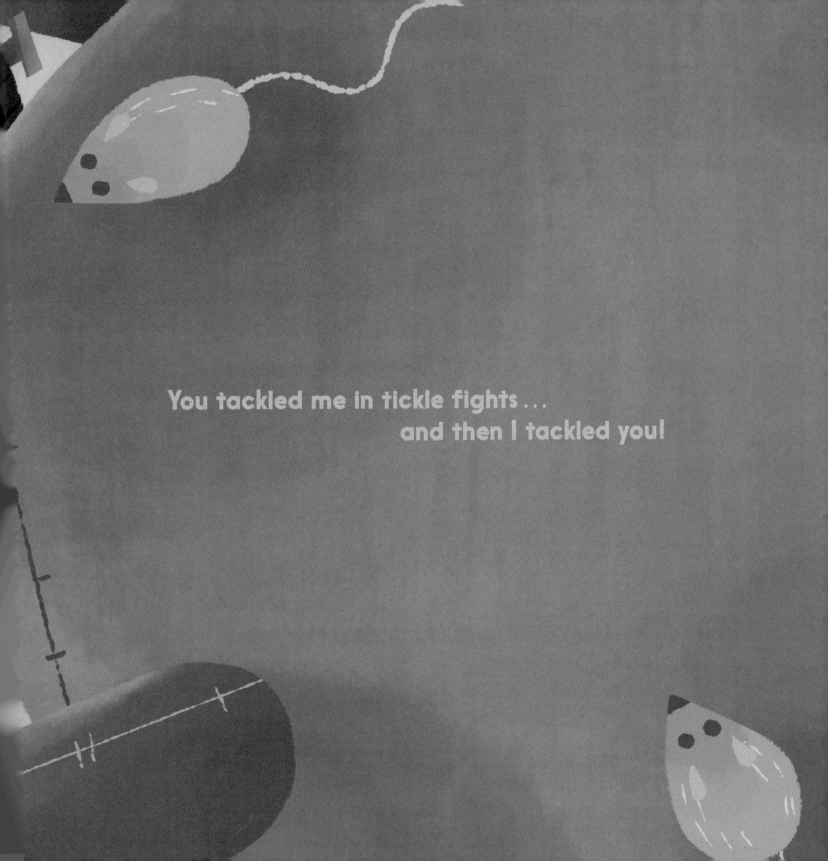

You tackled me in tickle fights...
and then I tackled you!

We galloped through a grassy field,
went fishing in a stream,

and when it came to making noise
we made a mighty team.

The secret hideout that we built
                was awesome to behold.

My face turned red with laughter
from the silly jokes you told.

You kept a sharp-eyed lookout
as you rode upon my back.

We worked up mammoth appetites
and gobbled down a snack.

But now the day has ended, and
the moon shines overhead,

so jump into your jammies, and
I'll chase you into bed.

Your fearsome yawns won't frighten me,
I'll hug you strong and tight,

then gently tuck you into bed
while whispering . . . good night.